MW00950641

Copyright © 2015 by CASA of Mesa County. 714536

ISBN: Softcover   978-1-5035-6926-3
        Hardcover   978-1-5035-6927-0
        EBook   978-1-5035-6925-6

Print information available on the last page

Rev. date: 05/13/2015

To order additional copies of this book, contact:
Xlibris
1-888-795-4274
www.Xlibris.com
Orders@Xlibris.com

or

CASA of Mesa County
www.AChildsVoice.org
970-242-4191
info@casamc.org

Lily was 7 years old when she came to live with her foster family. Her home before was not a safe place for Lily.

When she first saw the big white house at the end of the street where she would be staying, Lily was afraid. The house looked nice and there were kids playing in the street, but Lily felt her tummy tighten and her throat get dry.

Who would be in this house? Would they be nice? Would she have food? Would she have her own bed?

Lily clutched her blanket. It was one of the few things she had been able to bring with her. The torn blanket still smelled like her mom's perfume.

Lily missed her mom.

Lily's case worker, Ms. Kim, pulled into the driveway. Standing at the door was a smiling lady holding a round-faced baby in her arms.

As Lily got out of the car, the smiling lady came to her side. "Welcome, Lily, I'm Penny and this little guy is Jacob." She smiled a big smile and Lily felt the knot in her tummy go away.

Lily didn't feel as scared anymore.

Lily had been in her foster home for two weeks. She liked it there with her foster mom Penny and her foster dad Tom.

Lily still missed her mom and sometimes when she woke up at night she forgot where she was. Sometimes she would cry for her mom at night before she fell asleep.

One day Lily was eating a bowl of macaroni and cheese at the kitchen table. There was a knock at the door and her foster mom went to answer.

After a few minutes Penny came into the kitchen with another lady who was dressed in a bright red shirt. She had short dark hair and a big smile.

Lily liked her dangly gold earrings.

"Lily, this is your CASA," said her foster mother.

Lily didn't know what a CASA was. Was this lady a teacher? Was she a doctor? Or was she someone who was going to take her to a different home? Lily felt her tummy tighten again and she started to get worried.

The CASA knelt down beside Lily. "Hi Lily, my name is Joan. I bet you're wondering what a CASA is, huh?"

Lily nodded her head yes and looked down. She didn't feel like talking.

"CASA stands for Court Appointed Special Advocate," said Joan. "That's a long name, isn't it?"

Lily watched as Joan the CASA reached down in the bag she was carrying. She pulled out something that looked fuzzy and had spots.

"Lily, this is Chance the Cheetah," Joan said as she held the stuffed animal. "Chance and I are here to make sure you are safe."

CASA Joan handed the cheetah to Lily.

Lily grabbed his soft fur and held him to her cheek. Chance smelled like chocolate chip cookies and Lily giggled. CASA Joan smiled at Lily.

"Chance gets to stay here with you and I get to come visit you every month, Lily, because we have a very important job. Our job is to make sure everything is going good for you here in your foster home, and at school. Our job is also to make sure you are getting help if you need it. Does that sound ok?"

Lily looked at Joan and noticed how kind her blue eyes were. She shook her head and said "Yes," quietly.

Lily hugged Chance.

"You know, Lily, anytime you feel sad or scared you can talk to Chance, and when I come to visit you can tell me too. We care about you and we are here to listen."

Lily noticed her tummy didn't feel tight anymore. She would like to be able to tell Chance what she was feeling and she was glad she would be able to hold him at night when she felt sad and missed her mom.

Lily was also glad she would have CASA Joan to talk to. Her smile made Lily feel safe.

"Can Chance and I see your room, Lily?" CASA Joan asked smiling. Lily reached out her hand to CASA Joan.

The two walked toward the stairs leading to Lily's room.

Lily smiled at her CASA and knew that she wasn't alone anymore.

46416418R00015

Made in the USA
San Bernardino, CA
06 March 2017